The Color of
New York

JOSEFINA FONTANALS MARTÍ

iUniverse, Inc.
New York   Bloomington

The Color of New York

This is a work of fiction. All of the characters, names, incidents, organizations, and dialogue in this novel are either the products of the author's imagination or are used fictitiously.

iUniverse books may be ordered through booksellers or by contacting:

iUniverse
1663 Liberty Drive
Bloomington, IN 47403
www.iuniverse.com
1-800-Authors (1-800-288-4677)

Because of the dynamic nature of the Internet, any Web addresses or links contained in this book may have changed since publication and may no longer be valid. The views expressed in this work are solely those of the author and do not necessarily reflect the views of the publisher, and the publisher hereby disclaims any responsibility for them.

ISBN: 978-1-4401-9478-8 (pbk)
ISBN: 978-1-4401-9479-5 (ebk)

Printed in the United States of America

iUniverse rev. date: 1/22/2010

In memory of my father, the most intelligent man I ever knew. He was ahead of his times and instilled in me the importance of learning, especially languages.

I wish to thank The New School University, especially the teachers Barbara O'Brien, Ethel Owens, Carla Stevens, Elaine Edelman, Pearl London, and John McDonald Moore, for the wonderful educational experience I received.

Also, gratitude to my friend and copy editor in Barcelona, Carolyn Law, and my niece, Eva Fontanals, who encouraged me to publish this book.

This material for this book was written in Manhattan during the 80s. It is a collection of short stories, poetry, and a part of my diary which I wrote in New York before returning to Barcelona.

Now, in the year 2009 I have decided to publish these pieces and communicate with others the experiences I had in Manhattan for so many years.

Looking back I realize how different life in Barcelona and New York was, but the adventure was truly worthwhile.

Barcelona, 7 October 2009 *Josefina Fontanals*

The desire to write is the need to express oneself in writing. So one has to be oneself... and next... one must be true to oneself.

As a writer your first discipline is to be alive to everything. Here and now you begin to exercise and sharpen your five senses: touch, sight, hearing, scent, and taste.

— Anaïs Nin

A Doll's Apartment
in the Year 2000!

(Written in 1980. Based on Ibsen's play *A Doll's House*.)

A Doll's Apartment <u>in the Year 2000</u>!

A One Act Play

SCENE ONE: 8:00 a.m. – <u>IN THE YEAR 2000</u>

SCENE TWO: THAT SAME EVENING

CHARACTERS

NORMAN: 37-year-old husband of Hedda. Tall, handsome, and very macho-looking.

HEDDA: 32-year-old wife of Norman. Small, feminine and fragile-looking.

SETTING

A STUDIO APARTMENT IN A BROWNSTONE ON THE EAST SIDE OF MANHATTAN. A HUGE LIVING ROOM WHICH INCLUDES A SOFA BED, A KITCHENETTE, AND DINING ROOM SEPARATED BY A SCREEN AND PLANTS. SPARCE FURNITURE AND EMPTY SPACES, BUT COMFORTABLE AND COZY.

SCENE I

Eight o'clock in the morning, in the year <u>2000</u>. A wall clock shows the time. The sofa bed is unmade and some breakfast dishes are in the sink. The room is untidy.

 HEDDA is leaving the house and saying goodbye to her husband. She is wearing a very formal tailored suit and is carrying a large briefcase. She looks like a busy, stern executive, wearing glasses and carrying the morning newspaper under her arm.

 NORMAN is still wearing pajamas and an apron. He is drying his hands, wet from washing dishes. He smiles tenderly at Hedda, who looks somewhat absent minded and in a hurry. He kisses her.

HEDDA: Goodbye, darling. I will be late for dinner tonight, I have two meetings with the other bank directors.

NORMAN: I will be ready and waiting for you. Today I am cooking moussaka for dinner. I got the recipe from the Greek owner of the Excell Coffee Shop.

HEDDA: How cute my little squirrel is. How he knows what pleases his wife!

NORMAN: Hedda, I will need some money to buy food.

HEDDA: What happened to the fifty dollars I gave you yesterday?

NORMAN: Darling, we had fourteen guests yesterday for cocktails. I had to buy the drinks, and dates with nuts, and other goodies.

HEDDA: Oh, Norman! We shouldn't spend all the money I earn as the director of two banks, you know? I don't think I will be promoted forever.

NORMAN: But, Hedda, I'm very careful about not spending money on the house-keeping. I bake the bread myself and make the jelly, and I do all the cleaning and washing in the house without anyone to help me. We used to have a servant, remember? And you didn't want him around because you prefer me to take care of everything. And yet, you are not pleased?

HEDDA: Dear Norman, what a sweet featherhead you are... You are seducing me, as usual. Come, come and kiss me. (They kiss. Hedda fumbles in her attaché case.) Here, I'll give you $25 for today's expenses.

Maybe we could have Retsina wine with the moussaka tonight. Be careful, Norman, you are a sweet little spendthrift, But you are getting to be a very expensive darling man!

NORMAN: Thank you, thank you, Hedda. I love you so much.

HEDDA: Goodbye, Norman. See you at dinner time.

NORMAN: Goodbye, Hedda! Don't work too hard. Did you take the papers for the meeting? I left them ready for you near your briefcase.

HEDDA: Yes. I don't think I forgot anything.

NORMAN: Your silk scarf! I ironed it yesterday.

HEDDA: Oh, yes, I nearly forgot it. (Norman gets the scarf and hands it gently to Hedda.)

NORMAN: Goodbye, Hedda. Will you call me from the office as usual?

HEDDA: Yes, I will, sweetheart.

Hedda leaves the house as Norman waves goodbye to her from the window.

When he sees her disappear from sight, he looks at the clock and his cheerful look instantly changes to one of worry. Constantly looking at the clock, he rushes around the room tidying up, making the bed and turning it into a sofa, and washing some dishes which are still in the sink. He gets the vacuum cleaner out of the closet and vacuums the floor. His arms and legs have tried to do everything at once, like the blades of a windmill. He finally collapses, breathless, on the sofa.

SCENE II

Same living room. The house is very clean and tidy now. Norman and Hedda are finishing their dinner at a well-set table including a bouquet of red roses and two lighted candles. An empty bottle of wine is on the table.

Norman, wearing an elegant dark suit, is very dressed up for the occasion. It is a week before their tenth wedding anniversary, but today they are celebrating it privately. Hedda is looking radiant: long black dress, expert makeup, and blonde hair loose.

NORMAN: My day has been much worse than yours, Hedda, and I never complain. Going to work at the office and having meetings all day is not as tough as it seems. It gives you an outlook on the world at least. I wish I had the opportunity to get out of the house a little bit more.

HEDDA: Norman! How can you say such things! You don't know what a struggle we women have as breadwinners. Besides, for men it's fun to spend their time squandering the wife's money all day—while she works endless hours. And you do get out of the house. After all, you went shopping, didn't you?

NORMAN: Oh, Hedda! I had a terrible experience on my way back from the supermarket this morning.

HEDDA: What happened, dear?

NORMAN: I accidentally ran into a bunch of crazy women who surrounded and humiliated me...

HEDDA: Why did they humiliate you? What did they do to you, darling?

NORMAN: The usual. What they always do on the street when they see a man. They cannot go by without following and throwing a compliment at him. But, good God! What flattery! I felt so humiliated and ashamed that I think I blushed clear to my feet.

HEDDA: Norman, tell me. Tell me! What did they say?

NORMAN: Dear Hedda. I don't even dare mention it. It is so humiliating for a man to have to hear such things.

HEDDA: I will not let them do this to you. I will pull the hair out of their heads until they have to wear wigs for the rest of their lives!

NORMAN: One of those women who followed me said: "Sweety pie, how much I would love to eat you for dessert today."

HEDDA: Good God! How fresh! What did you answer?

NORMAN: Nothing at all. I didn't look at the woman. I just stared at the ground and tried to ignore that moronic group of women following me.

HEDDA: Couldn't you get away from them?

NORMAN: No such luck. I tried to go faster and faster, but I couldn't run because the shopping cart was loaded heavily with the groceries. It was awful. They followed me for a long while. For a moment I thought I was going to be raped...

HEDDA: (Laughing) That would have been fun, Norman. We could have sued them afterwards and spent the money on champagne.

NORMAN: (Looking very grim.) Hedda! Don't take it so jokingly. The role of the man is painful in the modern family. I preferred the patriarchal time when...

HEDDA: (Suddenly very serious and stiff.) Now, Norman, darling, don't start all that nonsense all over again. You know very well that the past is gone forever and, luckily, we can't return to prehistoric times... Let's change the subject... Norman, what dance are you going to perform for our anniversary celebration a week from now? They are all eager to see it.

NORMAN: I thought I had best consult you first. Your advice is always necessary for me.

HEDDA: What about that bolero suit in which you performed so successfully several years ago. Remember? You wore very tight black trousers and a shirt with enormous wide sleeves and that glorious red waistband.

NORMAN: Well, I thought I would do something new this time. I don't dare tell you, but I have been practicing a new dance while you were at work. It is a secret I have been keeping.

HEDDA: Oh, Norman, please, please tell me! I am so curious!

NORMAN: (Shyly and blushing.) Well, remember when we went to Seville three summers ago and we saw the *corridas* and the flamenco gypsies dancing? I was so fascinated by them that I bought a flamenco record and have been learning the "zapateado".

HEDDA: What is the "zapateado"?

NORMAN: A Spanish flamenco dance where the man kicks the floor rapidly with his heels. I could wear the same trousers and the red waistband as in the Bolero dance. I would only need to buy a polka dot shirt.

HEDDA: (Hesitatingly.) I don't know, darling, if you should spend more money...

NORMAN: (Cunningly.) Please, Hedda...

HEDDA: All right. I will buy a new shirt. But you should start practicing soon and I will watch you. Sometimes you dance too fast.

NORMAN: You will be proud of me, Hedda. You will see.

When Norman is trying to show his wife the bolero garment, the play is interrupted by the audience, who start screaming and shouting.

There is a big uproar.

Some spectators climb towards the stage and try to grab Hedda. The bolero garment and the flamenco hat are torn and smashed by the angry mob. It is impossible to enact the third scene.

A crying director finally appears on the set. It takes him 15 minutes to appease the crowd. Finally he mumbles:

Sorry, sorry, gentlemen and... ladies. With profound grief we have to end this performance because of the impossibility of silencing the audience. We beg your pardon for having dared to change Ibsen's play, *A Doll's House*, into *A Doll's Apartment*. It was an experiment that failed. It was a mistake. We will close today's play *A Doll's Apartment* and reopen with the original play *A Doll's House*, by Ibsen. You can get your money back and return tomorrow, the 10th of October, 1979, to see Mr. Ibsen's play performed exactly as he wrote it.

(Applause and whistles)
Finally, the audience is happy.
CURTAIN

TO BE A HOUSEWIFE

I never wanted to have children of my own. No dogs, no cats, no pets. And look at me now. Three daughters, a canary, an awful white poodle called Lilly and a cat, Roxy, who has spoiled all my furniture, drapery and curtains.

I am trapped. By a life that I didn't want. By a husband who is a macho, and by my parents who still treat me like a little child. I have always admired my younger sister. She is 38. I am three years older than she. And trapped. Trapped in a house like the old black cotton slaves.

Rushing, rushing, alarm clock at 6:30. Breakfast, dishes, lunch, dishes, dinner, dishes and bed... no sleep.

I have a vital husband. He wants to have sex all the time, and he screams on every orgasm he has and several times the neighbors called the police thinking that he would murder me. But no, the screams are not only in bed but on the living room couch or in the bathroom. Whenever he can get hold of me.

I don't dare refuse his sexual urges. I was told that I have to fulfill a man's needs, through his stomach (I am an excellent cook) and further below.

But I hate cooking and am tired most of the time and lay like a dead body when he performs at night and shouts at me, "Rosario, why don't you scream? Move, move your body fast. Faster." And I try to obey him, but I cannot utter a sound. As a matter of fact, I try to act like a robot, sleeping, but pretending I am very awake.

What a life. A housewife. At first, marriage was fun. Carlos and I were in love. We met watching a show one evening. One of his girl friends was sick and I desperately wanted to see "The Rainbow." So I bought Carlos the extra ticket. Talk about destiny! But if this life is destiny, why should I always have the worst part?

Remembrances. My happy childhood. I was the clever girl. Always A+ in all my courses in college.

My sister was the pretty one. She was not so brilliant as I was, but she has been a beauty. Men surrounded her, and she was always laughing. She still is pretty and has the best sense of humor. No wonder that she keeps her optimism. She is free as a bird. She never married nor does she have children or pets. She can go any place she pleases, since she is a famous artist and earns enough money to support herself.

I have never been jealous of my beautiful younger sister. I was the ugly duckling in the family, since my older brother, Juan, is very handsome also.

I cannot get out of my trap. The chains are too thick. I cannot leave my children behind, nor can I take them with me since I would like to be free. And Carlos, he would commit suicide if I left him. I wouldn't care about the pets.

This is my last attempt to get out of this nasty life. I decided one Sunday, when I was almost ready to explode. It was a sunny day and I would have liked to be myself, to run in the park nearby and watch the birds flying and let my imagination go wild, and talk to each tree and flower and tell them I loved being free, writing, becoming a famous novelist, being free, on my own, no ties, no ties. No dishes, no cooking, no ironing, no washing.

To write, to write. "A room of one's own."

And I made the great decision. Nobody dared stop me. I left Barcelona on the 15 of September and registered at The New York School in New York for a fall semester. I want a degree in liberal arts. Take courses in writing, film and acting.

I will return home for Christmas. The family is still astonished at my decision. But they accepted my adventure, because they knew... they knew that I would always come back to them, and that nothing could change my mind.

Now, I write from my small room at the Eden House for Women.

I write, I write and I sleep so well at night!

A CRITIQUE OF
THE PLAY *HAMLET*

In reviewing the characters of the play Hamlet my sympathies go to Ofelia, because she is the main victim. Torn between her obedience to her father and her love for Hamlet, she resorts to her last recoil, the last solution, the schizophrenic divided mind: madness. She is no heroine, no Antígone; she only has assumed her role as a woman, the role that culture, society, has imposed upon us, the victims of our own deeds. She is not an Indira Gandhi, or a Margaret Thatcher, fulfilling her role as a human being. She is only a shadow, the shadow of her men, her foolish father and the ambiguous Hamlet. She is torn between the two, she doesn't assume any responsibility, she doesn't have the chance! Her madness is a solution to Hamlet's insecurity and doubt. For, if Hamlet had really loved her, she would never have gone mad, she would have been a Juliette, she would have mourned her father with grief, but the love of her man would have saved her from the last evasion.

Alas! How sad, anonymous, insignificant her madness was, compared to the powerful, rich and fulfilling madness of the hero, Hamlet! She is the one who should have been the ghost, the conscience of Hamlet, and tell him how crazy he was, not to accept a woman's love. She would have been the strongest if she had the chance, and helped Hamlet get rid of his doubts. But she could only obey her father and society and, although she probably wanted to obey Hamlet too when he sent her to a nunnery, she could not do so, it would have been too much for her. She was not worth to Hamlet's love: "Get thee to a nunnery!" he tells her as the last solution for her.

Luckily for Ophelia, she prefers to resort to a state of mind that we call insanity, rather than to obey Hamlet and shut herself up totally from life. At least, with the kind of madness she assumes she can sing and pick flowers and float for a while in the river, and mock a little her victimizers before she makes an elegant exit from this crazy world of men.

But neither is poor Hamlet to blame for society's contempt for women: "Get thee to a nunnery, go: farewell. Or, if thou wilt needs marry, marry a fool: for wise men know well enough what monsters you make of them."

Isn't this a prejudice against women that we accept without winking, the humiliations, the impositions, and the injustices of the negative feeling of men projected onto us?

Eve tempted Adam with an apple. We women need no ghost to tell us that we want revenge, the revenge of the injustices of men. Women are viewed, from the beginning of the Bible, as insidious serpents, as demons, tempting men and leading them to sins, to fornication, getting them out of their minds with seduction and promiscuity. Yet, who is promiscuous here, the one who asked always for the virginity of women, who stoned adulterous women, who paid prostitutes for their own pleasure?

Oh Hamlet, Hamlet, how much you have stirred the dormant demons who were in me, who still are in me when I hear you saying: "God hath given you one face and you make yourselves another; you jig, you amble, and you lisp and nickname God's creatures and make your want your ignorance".

Yet Ophelia accepts it all, like the universal mother every woman is, and praises Hamlet:

"O, what a noble mind's here o'erthrown the cortior's soldier's, scholar's, eye, tongue, sword: the expectancy and rose of the fair state, the glass of fashion and the mold of form, the observed of all observers, quiet, quiet down! ...That unmatched form and feature of blown youth blasted with ecstasy: O, woe is me, to have seen what I have seen, see what I see!

Oh Hamlet, Hamlet, how much I empathize with your thoughts, when I have been awakened to hear and to see how much all occasions do inform against women when I hear that in the middle ages men took time and intelligence (?) to discuss whether women had soul or not. We were the outcasts of society, the servants, the assistants of men. How much I cry out like you Hamlet when you say in anguish:

"How all occasions do inform against me, and spur my dull revenge! What is a man, if his chief good and market of his time be but to sleep and feed? A beast, or some craven scruple of thinking too precisely in the event... I do not know why yet I live to say 'this thing's to do', sith I have came, and will, and strength, and means, to do't."

Why, why instead of being passive females can't we say like Hamlet:

"Rightly to be great is not to stir without great argument, but greatly to find quarrel in a straw when honour's at stake. How stand I then... and let all sleep? ...O, from this time forth, my thoughts be bloody, or be nothing worth!"

FIESTA ON THE COSTA BRAVA

It is the *fiesta mayor* in the village, the big holiday of the year. The children are assembling wood for the bonfires. It is the hour when the sea and the sky exchange colors. The air is perfumed by the sea and the families gather to enjoy the *fiesta*.

On the terrace of the small bistro the tourists drink *sangría*: red wine with apples and fruits. They laugh and enjoy the peculiar holiday. They drink and drink, and laugh and laugh.

Carmen, the waiter's daughter, sits on the porch. She doesn't smile. She has a gypsy look—dark hair and dark skin. She is neatly combed and is wearing a silky ribbon and a blue dress. Her father is pouring jars of sangria for the tourists; her mother is busy in the kitchen.

Carmen looks at her new white shoes and socks. She is waiting to go with her parents to the *fiesta*.

No other children around, just herself and Punkie, her little dog, who is chained and sad, not allowed to bark.

The small girl is unaware of the reddened sky. Her imagination runs wild. She is not a gypsy girl anymore. She is a small lady in a white silver dress. Her parents don't need to work since they are rich. They don't live in the old village but in a mansion in a beautiful city. She is allowed to have cats and dogs, and a rabbit, a white rabbit named Jordi. She wears new white dresses and bows everyday and goes to all the parties in town and dances and dances, like other rich children. And Tomás, the boy next door, smiles and plays with her instead of teasing her and calling her gypsy girl.

The bonfires on the beach are being lit. Fireworks sweep the sky. The tourists drink more sangria, the waiter rushes from table to table, the woman prepares salads and sardines, rushing, getting ready in her mind for the *fiesta*. Men and women, young and old, all gather around the piles of wood.

The sound of the music and fireworks is dying down. There are only twinkling stars in the dark and a few silver lights falling over the ashes in the sand.

The small girl is now allowed to go with her parents to the remaining *fiesta*.

LETTER TO A SPANISH EXILE

Barcelona, 15 April, 1945

Dear Antonio,

    I hope that you get this letter somehow, since I know that it is difficult to get mail from Spain now, but I have the feeling this time that everything is going to work out and that circumstances will change, for the better.

    We miss you so much, and your girlfriend, Carmen, is always sad since you left us six years ago. She was upset because you would not take her with you. She would have left her parents and family in order to follow you in exile, and live all the dangers you are having. She doesn't share her parents' political ideas since she thinks that you are right, that your ideals are the right ones, and that you are not an atheist and Communist as they say, just because you disagree with their codes and norms and that you don't fit into their standards.

We frequently get together, Carmen and I, and talk about you. We have received your pamphlets and are organizing meetings and plan to distribute them carefully. It has been a difficult job since there are many disguised policemen that follow our activities. They know that you had been actively involved in the Republican Party before. Carlos was discovered when he was delivering a speech in the basement in Alfredo's house, and both of them have been jailed. We have not heard from them, but we are afraid that they will make them talk since there is no time limit set for their interrogation. It was better before, when it took only 48 hours of trial and they could be relieved. Now our friends are not sure that they can endure more than two days of torture. It takes too much training and discipline to be able to stand that without confessing. Juan did confess last month, and five of our compatriots were imprisoned. We cannot trust anyone now. Because food and goods are so scarce since the Civil War ended, many are ready to spy on us in order to get some money as a reward. Students are the ones to be most feared. Although you can find among them some of the most enthusiastic patriots who would give their lives in order to get freedom, some of them succumb to the pressures of the Establishment. The parents who would have fought gladly on the side of the Republicans, who had ideals of freedom and liberty and democracy, are those who now most look toward the security and promised land of the Franco regime, and criticize their sons for their revolt, clinging desperately to whatever material security they have achieved, after many years of hard work. They cannot understand how their sons, who haven't had to struggle hard like they have, who have an opportunity to go to the university, how they, despite all this, rebel against the Franco regime and prefer to have clandestine assemblies and discuss politics instead of enjoying life and getting culture.

We received your poetry and the beautiful book you wrote about Catalonia. I am glad that you were able to publish it in exile, even if it was translated. We are looking forward to seeing you soon, I feel that everything will work out fine and that you will be able to return to Barcelona and that your books and poems will be read in Catalan, without the danger of you being put in jail or your writing banned.

Dear brother, I feel this nightmare is not going to last forever and that there will be no such hatred or war between brothers in the future.

Take care of your health. How is your bronchitis? Carmen sends you her love; she hopes that you have received the letter she wrote you recently. She is trying hard to raise money in order to pay for the trials and the bails of our friends. We are doing the best we can, but the situation is not easy now.

Mother sends you her love; she hasn't written you recently because she is recuperating from a bad flu. But she is better now and is longing to see you coming home soon.

God bless you, my dear brother, and let us pray and hope for better times to come!

Your sister

María

1978: FREEDOM OR CONSTRAINT

Constraint: Lack of freedom. Freedom! The magic word, the utopia, the last of the attainable worlds. There are countries that have suffered from a dictatorship for many years. We lived with one for forty years in Spain. Constraint of thought, constraint of sex, constraint of vision. There was no way of escaping from it.

Four decades of fear and constraint in Spain! Fear of talking, thinking, having new ideas! The intellectuals were the ones who suffered the most. They were beaten up, tortured, killed because of their beliefs, their ideas of freedom. There was persecution of nationalist priests in the Basque Country, persecution of thought of independence in Catalonia. We were not allowed to speak our language, Catalan. It is a rich and melodic language and poets, writers, journalists had either to flee in exile or start writing in the official language: Spanish.

When the dictatorship in Spain died, new hope of freedom and democracy swept the country. For months, the awakening of freedom in people was like the waking from a long, long nightmare. But the spirit of freedom had never left these men and women and children who loved their country where they were born, who loved their language, their tradition, their folk songs...

A new Spain is slowly emerging into the world now. Now in Spain the emblems of the different banners symbolize the thoughts of the different Spaniards, united, yet with their idiosyncrasies. Now in Spain we talk about politics and discuss it and we can speak up and gather in groups, and fight for some justice. Now in Spain women unite for their rights and complain for the first time of the constraint that men have inflicted upon them for generations.

Now in Spain there is no fear of singing folk songs; now intellectuals, writers, poets can create without constraint, telling the world what they feel they have to tell.

Like a threatening cloud that suddenly vanishes into light, white smoke in the air, the ghost of constraint is beginning to fade, slowly, in the skies of Spain.

I USED TO BELIEVE IN ANGELS

I used to believe in angels at that time. I was in a fairy tale world, the world of my childhood.

When I lost a tooth, my parents always had a present, and told me that an angel had brought it for me. "Would you like to see him?" my mother whispered. As if in a trance, I would slowly open the door of the bedroom. I caught a glimpse of the angel sleeping in my parents bed, his head and body almost covered by the sheets, showing only the curls of his blonde hair (my mother's wig, naturally). But I would not approach him, for if I did he would fly away. The magic of these hours reinforced my fantasy.

But life is not always magical. Sometimes I had to wake up dramatically to reality.

I can recall the day of my first communion when I was six, since it is an important celebration for Catholics. I wore a long white dress, with a white veil that covered my head like a bride. There were two white angels with huge white wings, at each side of me, accompanying me to the altar. I felt like a Queen, floating in the air, loved by parents, relatives, and most of all, by Jesus.

When the ceremony was over and I was leaving the church, two little girls approached me and asked me for some prints. The girls were thin, very pale, and dressed in old, shabby, asylum uniforms. I recognized the two angels. To my amazement, these were the girls that had entered the altar with me. No more white wings, no more smiling faces, there was poverty and hunger in their looks.

I was sad for the rest of the day. The glamour had disappeared. It was a great disappointment, it was unknown to me that there could be unhappy and poor people around. But my sadness did not last long.

I was the oedipal girl in the family. I didn't realize it at the time, but I loved my father deeply, passionately, desperately. He was my hero, tall, handsome, and always nice to me. I was his favorite until my brother was born. Then I suffered from jealousy, the jealousy of a child! The frustration of having to share my father's love with my mother, sister and brother made me feel defeated in advance, the rivalry was too strong.

I was a child when my father died. I felt deceived. He deserted me, he didn't love me. If he had, he never would have left me. Alone and defenseless, I wept and wept, and turned myself to God. I loved God more than my father then. He had not deserted me, He was with me all the time, since his love for me was infinite.

Luckily, I am not a child any more. I am a woman now. I do not want to lose my capacity to love deeply, to become involved, to suffer, or be happy. In other words, to be alive.

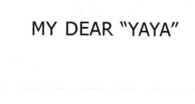

Everybody called her "yaya". It was a Catalan word for "grandmother." She died at 92, having been sick only one week; up until then, her health was good, although she had become completely senile in the last five years.

I was glad I had returned to Barcelona on that summer vacation in 1965 and could give my farewell to my "yaya". It was a tender farewell; I can recall the pink, lacy nightgown and her blue eyes, full of wit and wisdom, acquired from so many years of struggle and effort. By the time of her death, she was sweet and had developed a sense of humor that still amazes me now. Her senility disappeared the last week of her life, and she endured the last sufferings with a smile on her mocking face, as if it was all a big joke.

She had not been such a sweet and tender loving creature all her life. I was told that when she became a grandmother she softened to become the most loving "yaya" in the whole world. But she had had an austere and hard life, she had come from the poorest family in Valencia, and she had to work so hard all her life to have money enough to survive and care for her four children and husband. (She had run a room and board pension for thirty factory workers.) The tough life she led, the hard work she did for years had made her a harsh woman, who punished her children when in anger. My mother still has the scars on her head from a beating of my grandmother's. My aunt, my mother's sister, recalls her childhood with terror and tells how she frequently ran away in order not to get hit, then my mother received all the beatings, because she stayed stubbornly on the spot, refusing to run.

But I could never recognize in this picture the same person who was my "yaya", the loving, ever sacrificing grandmother who adored us all, and never ceased to love us forever. Whatever we did wrong, her grandchildren, she forgave; whatever she could give us, she gave us, never a thought of selfishness in her mind, never thinking about herself. It was a love that she gave us, that involved and surrounded us like an aura, a sense of being so much cared of, so much loved.

She lived always with my mother, despite the other children she had. I can recall her always staying in the house, always busy, sewing, washing, cooking, cleaning.

My grandfather had died when I was one year old; my mother has good memories of him. Yet, I recall my grandmother complaining that he was a gambler and that he frequently lost the money that she so laboriously had earned.

My grandmother was always saying that she could have written a book, the most interesting book about her life, since she had lived so much. But she did not know how to read and write. Poor people in Spain could not afford a school at that time. That was always a source of despair for her, because to be able to read is what she would have most liked. I will never understand how we, her grandchildren, living with her in the house, having received the most educated up-bringing with *Fräulein* taking care of us, speaking languages, studying thoroughly from our earliest childhood, how we, her grandchildren, never attempted to teach our dear yaya how to read and write; I will never understand that. Or why didn't my mother pay an instructor to teach my grandmother the essentials of reading? My mother had married a rich man, one of the most eligible bachelors, nineteen years older than she. Why, why didn't we make our grandmother happy by teaching her how to read and write?

"If I could tell the story of my life," she repeated to me frequently, "it would be the most interesting story. I have lived so much!"

Before marrying my grandfather, she had a rich suitor who had wanted to marry her. She almost accepted, wanting to get rid of the miserable life she had had in her childhood, when she and her sisters and brothers had frequently been hungry. But my grandfather, who also wanted to marry her at that time, said, "If you marry that man I will kill you first and then I will kill myself." So, she definitely married my grandfather.

She always told me stories of her life that would have fit more into a fiction book than into a real life; yet they were true stories, she did not invent them.

I remember her melodious voice. She must have also been a beautiful woman with blond hair and such shining blue eyes. She used to sing at parties when she was young, a crowd gathered around her while somebody played the guitar. Her voice and songs were still nice when she was in her eighties. But she was not an opera singer, nor a well-known soprano. She was simply a dutiful housewife, who loved to cook and take care of all of us.

I recall hearing her small steps in the early mornings when I was a child. It was always the same routine, getting up at 5:30 to fix our breakfast before we went to school. It took her a long time to prepare our breakfast. In the old times nothing was easy. The fire in the stove had to be lit, and then the coffee had to be ground by hand in an old fashioned wooden grinder that made a noise that woke us up in the morning.

The everlasting sound of her steps got more tired when the evening came. Then she used to sit in the living room sewing, her feet under a brazier that warmed up the whole room. She was never alone, somebody always joined her in the afternoons, and it gave a feeling of coziness and warmth to always have the yaya around the house.

The "yaya"! Everybody called her so, even the men who came once a month to bring coal for the stoves. Or others who made weekly deliveries of red wine or olive oil carafes or other goods. All these men never left the house without being invited to some cookies and a glass of sweet wine. She was worried when she was out of cookies, - "What shall I give the electrician who is coming to fix the lights today?"- But she always could find something.

What she enjoyed most was going to the market everyday. They all knew her, the butcher kept the best pieces for her. The women who sold fish gave her the freshest fish that still smelled of sea when she brought it home.

Her breakfasts when she returned from the market were real banquets: sausages, tomato spread over the bread, sardines, and always, up until a week before she died, a glass of red wine.

Her customs were simple. She never smoked, or drank other alcohol except that glass of wine in the morning. She never wore make-up or had any social life. Her dresses and her shawl were also black, contrasting with her white hair, rolled in a small knot in the back. It was the custom at that time that women past fifty (or even earlier) would always dress in black, since they had a relative or husband or son to mourn, so they never stopped mourning.

How different grandmothers are nowadays! They dye their hair, wear different colors, and the mourning black has disappeared. They are not called yayas anymore.

The only time I can recall my yaya wearing a color different from black was when she was sick, the last week of her life. The pink colors she wore made her look sweeter. Her blue eyes full of wit and her peaceful smile stood out when she was all dressed in pink.

If I mourn her — the yaya I loved so much, the yaya who loved me so much — the color of remembering her will never be black but pink, the color she wore on the last days of her life.

A PLACE I LOVED AS A CHILD

I remember it quite vividly now. It was buried in my mind, since it was very long ago. It is one of the memories I have now, when I think about my childhood.

I was seven years old. We had rented a house in the country, like every summer, in the mountains, near the Pyrenees.

I remember the fields, the fresh grass, the cows pasturing leisurely nearby.

It is the smell of green cut grass that I remember most.

I like the crisp days of September! The air was cool in the afternoons. The poppies seemed like red butterflies flying in the meadows. I recall playing in the fields, among the small wild flowers, violet and yellow. It was the scent of spring, of autumn, of winter and summer, all at once.

We played in the fields, the cows gazing at us, indifferent and drowsy, while we ran wildly in the hills. My sister and I used to play hide-and-seek, and we were so small at that time that we could easily hide in the wheat grass. The green meadows moving under the breeze, like a huge green sea. I recall the yellow and red colors of our dresses, floating in the air, contrasting with the blue of the sky. I remember how much we ran, and rolled downhill, laughing happily.

We didn't dance, but all my memories seem to be associated with a wild dance in the meadow fields, or in the woods. Why do I so often imagine dancing in the woods? Feelings of being in some enchanted garden, with gnomes and dwarves dancing with me. A world where I had wings and was flying in the air. The daydream of every child: To fly, to leave the earth, to be lifted in the air by strange forces that defy the strong force of gravity.

Oh, yes! My childhood was a very happy one.

POETRY

Poetry, which is our relation to the senses, enables us to retain a living relationship to all things.

— Anaïs Nin

OTHER GUERNIKAS (1979)

No furious brush strokes
No genius to shake us
No happy dances
But the soft falling
Of the dead.
No music
but the blasts of gunfire and grenades.
No students
but apprentices
of the skill
to kill.
Poets and peasants
hiding in the jungle
fighting for their
Beloved.
Mothers, clutching their babies,
running
from the savage crowd.

And other Gods
never sleep
and guaranty

Wealth
to the respectful
to the good ones.
They sweep away
the disturbing young
with new methods of
Fumigating
the irritant insects.

In the end
technique always wins.
Peace is restored in Nicaragua.

THE DELACORTE CLOCK IN THE ZOO

A clock of dancing creatures,
the banging of the time.
The dancing starts,
the bear, the rhino, the penguin
all around the clock.
Bing beng, bing beng!
Dancing around and around.

Blue waters glittering in the pond
and the baby seal
following the rhythm of the dance.
Children staring at the gigantic gorilla,
shouting to make him laugh,
but the gorilla doesn't budge.
He sees only the food.
He doesn't want to dance.

FROM THE POSTCARD
"BROKEN DISHES"

My four brothers and I gathered in the
dining room,
all clean and tidy, hands carefully washed,
the baby smiling in the cradle,
waiting for the feast to come.
Fragrances of sweet potatoes,
puddings and cranberry sauces
entered from the kitchen next by.
My mother was sitting near us,
radiant in her blue new dress.
She had prepared that dinner with so
    much care.
Saved money for months, working as a
    cleaning woman.
Father had been fired from his job long
    ago.

Mother was staring at the clock
hearing in silence its tic-tac.
Her hands crossed over her lap
as if praying for some miracle to come.

Suddenly the entrance door opened
  loudly.
My father appeared, tall and big as ever,
his face red, disheveled and unshaved.
He mumbled something, stared at us,
at the table, so nicely set.
The shining silver, plates and glass.
"What is this!" he shouted. He gazed at
  my mother.
"You have a lover who paid you this."
In a rage he snatched and tore my
  mother's dress.
We all started to cry.
This time the belt was not for us.
Father grasped the tablecloth from one
  end of the table.
Dragged it along the floor.

I will never forget that Christmas
the broken dishes, scattered around.

CENTRAL PARK

Little blond angels
spreading their navy blue wings,
climbing the Alice in Wonderland statue,
listening to the Ugly Duckling story.

Little black angels
climbing over Anderson's statue,
knocking him with fists
trying to tear his nose out.

Joggers running wild.
Squirrels made blind
by little angels in the park.

ON A BENCH IN CENTRAL PARK

It is autumn.
A mild breeze refreshes the air.
An old woman
dragging her poor belongings
rests on a bench in Central Park.

She is alone in the world
No place to go
No room
No bed.

A squirrel runs suddenly
to her side
and waits
sitting on her tail.

The old woman smiles,
browsing in her paper bag
she spreads some crumbs
on the grass.

A myriad of little creatures
surround her.
She is no longer alone.

Children are running
and laughing around.
The red and golden trees
sway their branches.

She is not homeless.
Has the sky as her roof.
She is the owner of
the park.
No landlord can kick her out.

HOW TO BUY A LAUNDROMAT

"Turn coins into cash"
the ads says
"You can earn $ 22,000
a year or more
while you spend the time
else where.
In this seminar you will earn
how to attract customers", etc

Yes, I will save money to
attend this seminar,
later to buy a Laundromat.
My clothes will always be
clean and dry.
No more working in this black
underground.
I will enjoy being rich
giving refined dinner parties
inviting nice girls to dance.
The machines will do all

the job for me
while I am having a
wild time.

"Stop your daydreaming, Billy.
Let us fix these pipelines.
Boss told us if we don't do
it fast
someone else will do the job for us."

DESCRIBE AN AUTUMN LEAF

I closed my eyes
and felt the leaf.
I was blind,
and even as the blind
sense those they love,
I touched and touched.

It was not soft.
It was not warm.
I felt the nerves.
Like thin paper
it crumpled
as when a written page
is of no use.

But, never mind,
describe, describe!
Do I smell this dead leaf?
Be specific. Don't play around.
My senses
are numb from so much
sleeping alive.

But, let us proceed,
what is left behind?
Oh yes, the sight, the sight!
Let me look at this leaf again
as if it was under a microscope.

What do you see?
I see a dead leaf,
twisted and ugly,
the color of spoiled burgundy wine.

Good Lord! Forgive me,
but this is all.
I do not like this leaf.
It is dead
and will fade away
when winter comes.

AUTUMN IN CENTRAL PARK

Yellow, red silhouettes
dancing
showing off their bright design.
White, crystal forms
dropping from the sky
joining the ballerinas
with their rhythmic drums.
The laughing
is becoming wild.
But jealous clouds
send violent winds
that swirl the dancers
in a crazy waltz.

The ballet is over now.
Softly all rest
in a red and yellow coffin
that scents the earth
with new seeds
to come.

A PHOTOGRAPH OF EVALYN
WHEN SHE WAS SEVEN YEARS OLD

When my younger sister Evalyn
was seven years old
she was a very pretty little girl
that looked like a doll.
Golden curls and blue eyes.
She was called "Miss Diagonal",
the promenade where
nice children walked
on Sunday
with their nannies.

But she was not a happy child,
always so clean and tidy.
I knew how she hated
her blue organdy dress,
and how much she would have liked
to play in the mud
with naughty boys
in the park
and be a runaway child
and join a circus

and join the clowns
and never again
be called "Miss Diagonal".

ICARUS

It took me a long time to see them build.
First the metal to support them.
The feathers were last,
smooth and light
like an angel's touch.

People gathered in the field,
curious to see me fly.
They had told me
that I would not survive.
I was scared, I didn't want to die.

Slowly I was gliding in the grass,
my feet still tied to the earth.
There was a mild clapping
as I began to rise.

High up in the blue
I was saluted by the swinging birds.
My plumage glittering in the silver
and orange shades.
Once above the clouds
I followed the white lines of

the jets,
greeted the rainbow.

Suddenly something rattled, noisily.
I woke up
My wings were gone.

AN ARTIST AT WORK

The Lord tells me:
"I have created the earth,
go and paint it."
I protest:
"Sire, I am out of practice."
"You can do it," he says.
"Sire, on the other planets,
there are no colors.
Why paint this one?"
"I want it to look different."

Loaded with brushes
and canvasses,
I travel around the world,
spreading green over fields
and mountains,
blue over skies
and oceans.

Starting with the North Pole,
almost freezing to death,
I paint everything white,
icebergs, hills, rocks.

The bears try to run away
from my brush.

In the spring,
small flowers
begin to appear
among the grass
asking me to do
their make up.
I sprinkle their petals
yellow, purple, violet.
Poppies like only scarlet.

Too warm to work during the summer,
I go to the "Costa Brava"
for a vacation.
Amused, I transform the ocean
into rose, iris, emerald.

Thunderstorms inspire me.
Watching the rising waters
I change the blue
into dark gray,
spray with white
the foam
that crashes
against the cliffs.

Winter and summer

blend into autumn.

I fly over the forest
drawing still lifes
of gigantic blossoms
competing with yellow
and red.

Bored I go to the desert,
mix all my pigments
to capture the texture
of the sand.
The camels try to run away
from my brush.

In the blaze of noon,
I cover the dunes
with gold,
orange at sunrise,
black at night.

ART AND PSYCHOLOGY

According to Dr. Otto Rank, professor of Art and Psychology, the artist is primarily an individual who is unable or unwilling to adopt the dominant ideology of his age, whether religious, social or other, not because it differs ideologically from his own, but because it is collective. For out of the conflict with collective ideas is born the tension which enables us to renew our ideas and forms.

In her book, *The Novel of the Future*, Anaïs Nin says that the future novel will have to learn to deal with the many new dimensions we have opened onto in the personality of man. She says the writer acts upon his environment by his selection of the material he wishes to highlight. He is, ultimately, responsible for our image of the world and our relation to others... At present we know more about ourselves just as we know more about the universe.

She continues, "Nowadays we have more to synthesize, and with psychology we have realized that the most important part of man, the psyche, was invisible to the naked eye. We have to include the expansion of the universe and the new power of communication which has progressed much faster than our power of assimilation and synthesis. This demands an even stronger, more flexible individual core than in the past.

"We have to overthrow frigidities towards the unfamiliar, the unknown, the unexplored, a prejudice towards experiment in the art of writing. We should always remain open to innovation.

"Depth alone is what gives perspective to the universal."

SOME REFLECTIONS ON FREUD

In Freud's age, the awful secret was sex. Today, it is spirituality. People today will discuss anything but their inner life.

— Ira Progoff

Before entering into criticism of Freud, we should, as with other philosophers or men of genius, see all the circumstances that surrounded them.

Dr. Levy states in his lectures that we must get deep into the theory that was developed by Freud and take into account that, because of the field of sexuality which Freud so emphasized, the detractors of his school have been more numerous than those of any other discoveries.

Even the closest pupils of Freud, who were among those who most ferociously attacked his theories, like Jung and Adler, had to recognize that, without the great discovery of the unconscious that Freud made, their schools of thought would not have been possible, since they were based precisely upon Freud's theories.

I think that a more eclectic approach might be useful to us if we try to understand each of these great men, individually, and bring together their points of view, which can be valid for each individual differently, and try to get the most enriching aspects from them. Sometimes ignorance (and envy, alas!) is what makes criticism of these men an unjust and superficial endeavor.

Freud was human, he was not God, he did not know everything. He was criticized, expelled, rejected by some of his dearest pupils. He was living in a very puritanical era and was quite puritanical himself. He had to battle against a hostile world of people who were frightened, in those times, to talk about sex, and doctors who were upset about his teachings.

Also, we should give further thought to the feminists' complaints about Freud's theories. In those days the role of woman as integral human being had not been accepted. She was primarily considered as lovable mother figure, or a tempting Eve—both myths that have made men fear her irrationally and love her at the same time. No wonder Freud, as a man of that time, and being involved totally in attempting to cure the sick by his therapeutic technique, didn't have the prophecy of other more advanced men to understand the psyche of women.

I think Freud's mistakes were many, but they could be held against his own culture and upbringing. The sense of guilt differs from one civilization to another and Freud was the product of western civilization, which means that the good and bad had different values than in other countries. In the eastern world, for instance, the word evil is not connected with what we call badness, but with the revolutionary, the different, the unfamiliar. It is certain that the men who were explorers or discoverers of the mind had to face great resistance, since it is easier to be adventurous in discovering countries or customs, or going to the moon, than in getting deep into our own mental life.

Eastern and western societies are broadening our field of information and expanding our intellect. Studies of the brain are advancing the field of psychiatry in such a way that it will surpass much of present knowledge of the mind. It is interesting to note the holistic approach toward the understanding of the human being that is emerging.

The merit of Freud was, first of all, to discover the unconscious, which exists in us as truly as the earth is round and, second, to work hard in finding a method to help people who are caught in the traps of difficulties which, at that time, not many persons were able to relieve.

THE LETTERS OF SIGMUND FREUD

Edited by Ernest L. Freud
Letter 277 Anonymous

Vienna IX
Beuggasse 19
April 9, 1935

Dear Mrs...

I gather from your letter that your son is a homosexual. I am most impressed by the fact that you do not mention this term yourself in your information about him. May I question why you avoid it? Homosexuality is most assuredly no advantage, but it is nothing to be ashamed of. No vice, no degradation; it cannot be classified as an illness; we consider it to be a variation of the sexual function, produced by arrest of sexual development. Many highly respectable individuals of ancient and modern times have been homosexuals, several of the greatest men among them (Plato, Michelangelo, Leonardo da Vinci, etc.).

It is a great injustice to persecute homosexuality as a crime—and a cruelty, too. If you do not believe me, read the works of Havelock Ellis.

By asking me if I can help, you mean, I suppose, if I can abolish homosexuality and make normal heterosexuality take its place. The answer is, in a general way, we cannot promise to achieve it. In a certain number of cases we succeed in developing the blighted germs of heterosexual tendencies, which are present in every homosexual; in the majority of cases it is no longer possible. It is a question of the quality and the age of the individual. The result of treatment cannot be predicted.

What analysis can do for your son runs in a different line. If he is unhappy, neurotic, torn by conflicts, inhibited in his social life, analysis may bring him harmony, peace of mind, full efficiency, whether he remains homosexual or gets changed.

If you make up your mind that he should have analysis with me—I don't expect you will—he has to come over to Vienna. I have no intention of leaving here. However, don't neglect to give me your answer.

Sincerely yours with kind wishes

Freud

DR. IRA PROGOFF
A TWO-DAY INTENSIVE JOURNAL WORKSHOP

Dr. Ira Progoff received his doctorate from The New School for Social Research in New York. He studied with Carl Jung who, along with Sigmund Freud and Alfred Adler, was considered one of the three pioneers of modern psychiatry.

Progoff says: "Particularly among creative people—from Leonardo de Vinci to Anaïs Nin—journal writing has historically been a vehicle for relieving tension, working through crises, and connecting with the intuitive, inner self."

He approaches anxiety from a completely wholistic perspective and views anxiety as a prerequisite to creativity.

"I would hope that the journal could be an important goal for a similar emphasis on psychological and physical self care. I have felt for a long time that many psychologists and psychiatrists are trained to rely too much on what one might call inappropriate psychological technologies—ways of taking over diagnosing and controlling psychological problems with drugs or electro-shock or whatever. I think good therapy is very often more a matter of helping someone who is stuck get unstuck. People are much more capable of guiding their own efforts to get unstuck than we've given them credit for.

The basic concept behind the journal method is that when you are having a hard time, when you are troubled, it doesn't mean that you are sick, it doesn't mean that you should immediately go out and put yourself under an expert's care. It may mean that you are in transition, that things are pretty confused for you right now, but that is all right. That is natural, it is part of the unfolding proves of life, as it moves from cycle to cycle."

In the 1960s, when LSD and other drugs were gaining popularity, Ira Progoff found himself invited to various meetings by people who thought he would favor such experiments.

"I told them that there were better ways to cultivate the imagination, ways that are organic to the psyche and did not bring the artificial.

In the Intensive Journal technique, there is room for orientations such as Zen, Psychosynthesis, psychoanalysis, yoga or whatever.

I like to describe it as a tool to help you deal with difficult times in your life, times of change or decision or loss—or great success for that matter.

Working in the journal can be a fulfilling experience in its own right, an art form if you like. It's something you can do just for the pure pleasure of it. You can play with it. Improvise."

EXCERPTS FROM MY DIARY

WRITTEN IN NEW YORK FROM <u>1978 TO 1990</u>

New York, September 1978

I was happily living in Spain in a world of family love and well being. I left all this behind. Now I am far away from my country, my friends. Changes again in my life, no rest.

New York — May

Spring in New York. The month of May. The flowers on Park Avenue contrast with the mountains of garbage because of the strike. The calmness of the city. No construction work today.

I saw the skyscrapers yesterday, gray in the rosy sunset. Such beauty could not be real.

I go to galleries, museums, films, and plays. But the movies of the streets, the artistic buildings, the dramas of the people's lives interest me more. Life is itself an art, the best most complete art. Life in its contrasts of hatred and love, sex and violence, beauty and terror.

New York — Tuesday

Walking in Central Park. The blossoms are not open yet. But the small buds are edging their way up through the underbrush and leaves.

The park is emptying, my steps sound like an echo. I am enjoying the walk. Yet, I also have a fear of crazy people. A jogger was recently murdered in a tunnel. I watch and try to follow the youngsters.

Today there is a crowd of children, most of them black, with kinky hair and big eyes. How much they enjoy the park! I see them climbing on the Hans Christian Andersen statue, over his head, hand, and back. The statue begins to look as if a big black cloud is surrounding it.

The colorfulness of this park! The black children, all eyes and mouth, laughing wholeheartedly.

A bit further up the hill, another group of small, white, well-behaved children in navy blue uniforms play in the park. How they run down the hill and laugh. I've seen them frequently, since the Lycee Francais is very near, and they go to the park for recess.

Today the Hans Christian Andersen statue has been cleaned. It does not have the red spray that someone painted on him one night. It was pathetic to see the statue all stained with red drops all over his face and eyes. It took away the world of magic the park evokes. I felt as if all the brutality on earth had burst onto his crying face.

Here the beauty of nature beguiles the violent instincts of men—that cosmic violence hidden behind the bushes, ready to explode.

Today the black children felt free from the hazards of life, and the rats that invaded their homes. Free from the darkness of their rooms.

How thoroughly they enjoyed climbing on the Andersen statue, banging his head, touching his face. The statue was unmoved, impassive, no longer crying red blood.

New York — The Barbizon

"The Barbizon Hotel for Women" at Lexington, 63rd Street.

Nice area, convenient place, subway nearby, buses up and down the Avenues.

Safe place, the "Barbizon Hotel for Women". Safe from the outside world. No men allowed in the hotel. Nice cafeteria, painted yellow. The food is good, and Jason, the waiter, likes me. In the morning, Emma, the colored waitress, has become nicer since she has gotten to know me better. "Have a nice day, sweetheart", she tells me when I leave the counter.

Breakfast at the Barbizon is surely not like breakfast at Tiffany's. There is efficiency at the counter. Emma is fast, she can carry ten dishes in both hand and arms.

Then there is Wanda, the waitress whose home was burned. We were asked for a donation. I gave her several dollars as a tip. Usually Wanda is there on Sundays, although she has moved to another apartment now near the one that burned. She comes from Brooklyn. What time must she get up? To be a waiter or waitress at the Barbizon or anywhere, what a task.

No days of wine and roses at the Barbizon. Ladies, in their eighties, decadent and lonely, speak of their past fame as dancers or actresses. They ask to be honored as they had been in the old days. How pathetic this is! Old glories, old deteriorated women, who will become eventually like babies. They hate to stay at the Barbizon, yet there is no other inexpensive place to go; they are stuck at the Barbizon for the rest of their lives.

Old ladies and young women, sharing their frustrations. The young women at the Barbizon are fighters. But they know in advance that they will never able to make it. "All I need is money," they tell me. "If I had an apartment, I could cook, I can't stand the Barbizon."

We are quite a group. A devastating, tragic ambiance is permeating the Barbizon. You can't escape it. You can't escape the neurotic syndrome from the time you get up. You hope the maid will come today and make your bed, which she is supposed to do every day. But as you listen to her complain about her sickness, and how she hates this place, you would like to tell her to go and take a rest.

You can't avoid the terror of this place when you enter the elevator. The woman in charge has to open the big, heavy doors. She can hardly do it, her feet are swollen from standing for such a long time.

The slaves in Greece or Egypt at least hopes for a better world, if they were lucky enough to be buried with their master's treasures. Here the gods are gone, only machinery and money are left. The power of money! You can see the lack of it as soon as you enter the Barbizon.

Some of the old ladies can hardly walk, sick and old as they are. Most of the young have no money, not even for meals. They work as clerks from nine to five, and hate their jobs. "Temporary" they say while they wait to be promoted. After work is over, they come back to the hotel tired and lonely. "I have to make it this time," they say. "I know I am talented, I just need recognition." Yet, the opportunity never arrives, they see their talents and youth wasted.

At the entrance to the hotel there are only two seats, which are always taken. There is the mezzanine and library, where one hopes to take a rest, and relax from the day. This is impossible, as some woman might be sleeping on the sofa with her shoes off.

There is a TV set on the 18th floor, but the women always quarrel about the selection of the program; you prefer to retire to your own room. You go up to your floor, but not before seeing two or three women walking around like ghosts, looking completely out of their minds.

I finally reach my room which is very small. It looks like a grave. I feel like a corpse. A grave with a bathroom, what a modern feeling. Of course, the room is not done, the bed neither.

You try to fight the depression by going for a walk outside, but the streets in New York depress you still more, with people talking aloud to themselves. The bus drivers are coughing, they sound as if they are dying. You feel as if you are in a hospital ward.

One woman singing loudly on the bus, quite unaware that she is not at the opera. Another, insults people who are sitting quietly next to her. She says Nixon is nuts! And the girl at the Playboy Club revealing her large bosom, at the club's entrance. You would not know whether she is dead or alive. A nicely dressed man at the store, with a smile painted on his face.

The lie of the American dream! The end of an empire. No more gods and myths, just survival. How can you avoid seeing the loneliness of the people, the slavery of working men converted into robots.

One should forget about this, at least momentarily, before going back into the cage of your room at the Barbizon.

New York — Monday

My next door neighbor, Mary, is in her room sleeping. When she comes from her work she goes to her room and sleeps. A good way to avoid facing problems. But I do not sleep. I am quite awake, watching around me, like a dog when he hears interesting sounds, his ears up. I watch and watch and think too much.

I am toxic from the smoke, from the air. I have become a machine, a polluted and rusty machine.

I went to Dr. Scholl because my feet hurt me. The old doctor was still there, the same as many years ago. He has grown old and has shrunk. He asked me at the end of his treatment whether I wanted a massage. I said yes, thinking naturally, he meant a foot massage.

But he got too enthusiastic and tried to reach too far up, until I had to stop him. I did it in a very polite way, getting his attention on my feet again.

He seemed to awake from a fantasy dream and I became very upset and disoriented. But my feet didn't hurt anymore and I could walk in the streets of New York again.

New York — October

The awakening of the city on a Monday morning. The life of this city, the bursting life. The explosion of the subway construction work, the maddening noises of the trucks. The rushing, the movement, the city at work. Cars and limousines, buses and subways rushing up and down.

Central Park. The color of each tree. It is as if a giant artist had painted the landscape with an artistic touch. A genius, going wild with his brushes and colors, painting the woods, the hills, the mountains. Brushing here and there, choosing the red in some trees, selecting the shade that matched its shape, like this elegant yellow Japanese tree near the lake, that scatters its precious fruits over the green carpet.

A mild breeze awakens the sleeping trees, shaking them softly. The flurry of yellow leaves, like yellow petals shining in the sun. The fragrance of wet grass. The rustle of dried foliage being crushed by footsteps in the park.

The Barbizon — Tuesday

The Barbizon Hotel for Women in New York City. It is called the House of Horrors. My small room. I have it crowded already with magazines, bulletins, books and dictionaries.

I try to clear my desk, it overflows with papers. There is no room left. I am afraid of becoming sick in this place. The terror of dying here, where your corpse would only be a nuisance and cost money. I have to overcome these thoughts. I do not have to panic, why should I get sick? I eat and sleep well. I do all the exercise I can, walking in the park, or in the country on week-ends.

I am lonesome and tired. I feel far away from my home in Barcelona, my family, my friends. My only refuge is the Barbizon, the substitution for my home. It is a poor and depressing replacement. My room is not done. I would like my bed made and everything tidy when I return "home". The maid is required to clean but disappears quite frequently. After a week of not appearing she wants to do my room. The only stimulation she gets is to do so when she sees the sign "Do not disturb" on my door which is usually when I am taking a shower. This really seems to trigger her sense of duty or curiosity. In five minutes the room is still full of dust, but the bed is finally made. I ask her timidly about vacuuming. "Oh that." she says absent mindedly. "The man comes once month." I do not insist. What for? I am glad at least she made my bed. I have the feeling I should be paid rather then pay for being in such a place. I stopped fighting for my rights a long time ago. I have become passive and submissive, expecting to be scolded at any time. "you should complain. You are paying for service.", my friends tell me.

The "Barbizon syndrome" gets you as soon as you enter this hotel, and it is contagious. Everybody has it. On the 19th floor instead of pianos and offices they should have a group of psychiatrists and psychologists treating us but, I am afraid, with no results, since they would be the first ones to fall into the Barbizon Syndrome!

New York – November

Walking, walking in the park in autumn.

Central Park, the womb of the world, the microcosm, a galaxy of its own. Squirrels getting fat, birds conversing softly, distant sirens, the laughter of children, footsteps crushing leaves in the grass. Shishkabobs, frankfurters, and cocacolas are sold from vendors' carts. The homeless drag their possessions in silence.

Pigeons surround a little boy. Children climb over the dwarves and giant mushroom of the Alice-in-Wonderland sculpture. Mothers hold their babies up to the little duck at the Anderson statue.

On the pond, large and small sailboats navigate leisurely, captainless, as if they were on the unbounded ocean. Autumn is coloring the trees and bushes with yellows, dark greens, blue greens.

Red leaves swirl in the wind.

Bees zoom among the flower beds.

New York — December

The night is dark, everything seems to sleep. I saw a dead man tonight. He was lying on the sidewalk like a package, an umbrella over him. A coat covered his face. A friend gazing without seeing, waiting. People gathered around him.

Today I noticed greater poverty than ever, misery, dirt. A pathetic young, unshaved man was looking in the street garbage cans for a few drops of beer. He frantically examined each can, like a dog – inhumane. And we, the passers by, fight proudly for human rights.

A beggar approached my table in Central Park and avidly took the buttered white rice than I had left aside. He didn't care about us seeing him, he was busy assembling the small portions of rice I had discarded from my lunch.

The homeless in New York! They are the faces of despair. Hungry, defeated, they sleep in the street like abandoned animals. The sick, the old, the poor, the battered, lost in the decline of life, mentally and physically deteriorating on the streets of New York. Trying to hold on to the last spark of life.

"No, don't give them money, Josefina. There are places for the homeless to go." Yes, a homeless residence, a refuge for delinquents and robbers. A haven for crime.

Winter in New York. Columbus Circle: a beehive community of cardboard boxes like a small town. In the cold winter I see them seek refuge in the entrances of buildings and subways.

When I am in my room at night, well fed and happy, resting under the blankets of a warm, cozy bed – I feel guilty and ashamed. Guilty for doing so little. Ashamed for not talking to them as friends. Friends of the human race.

New York — Winter

I go for a walk in Central Park. I walk endless with no sense of time. The tall trees are like white ghosts guarding the park. Icy drops land on the bushes.

The lake is a gigantic frosted mirror. Children are playing in the snow, throwing snowballs at each other. Red cheeks, eyes shining, the music of laughing children.

The clock at the zoo plays Christmas carols while the bear, zebra, penguin, and elephant dance around the hours of time.

Children are watching a gigantic gorilla trying to make him laugh.

The Anderson statue. A little boy climbs over the Ugly Duckling book.

A solitary duck, glides over the icy pond, searching for his lost companions.

The Alice in Wonderland statue. Children jump over the dwarfs and mushrooms, others reach Alice's head and swing over her hair.

I walk and walk. The squirrels watch me confidently with no fear. The beggars have disappeared. The baby seal is having his morning swim.

New York — August:
The Annual Women's Day Celebration

Yesterday I went to a Harlem church with my friend Anne. When we entered the church we were spellbound. I had never seen such a beautiful ceremony before. The parishioners were dressed up in their best Sunday outfits, their colored garments glimmered in the light. They were all clapping and singing. The children listened attentively. One girl had a red bow in her hair; it looked like a big red butterfly. A small child, in her mother's arms, was drinking from a bottle of milk while the mother followed to the rhythm of the music at the same time.

We were the only whites in the entire congregation, we sang and clapped as if we were part of the huge family.

An interesting young man was sitting in the choir. He was all dressed in black, which contrasted with the white tunics of the singers. I saw Anne looking at him attentively, as if she were bewitched.

Suddenly, this strange man got up and began talking in a harsh voice. I realized it was not a man. The black minister who spoke was a woman! Her hair was crisp and black as her face, suit and tie. Her speech was calm at first, then she got excited and her voice was like thunder.

We were all hypnotized, like snakes when they hear the sound of music. The woman minister continued shouting into the microphone. She screamed and gestured, talked and talked. Anne was in trance, absorbing every word she said, her teachings, her movements.

It was like a movie. A procession of women started walking slowly towards the altar, clapping and singing to the music. They were all dressed in white, with white hats on. Their bosoms were like big white balloons. It looked as if suddenly they were going to fly, big angels with their hats on.

The ceremony lasted several hours, but it seemed a short time to me. When it was over, we were invited to the reception downstairs. They all greeted us, their teeth shining as they smiled. They offered us cake and apple juice, and asked us about our different countries.

I was exhilarated. It was the "Annual Women's Day Celebration", a black woman was a preacher, and there was still faith on this earth. Life was not all frustration and despair.

Anne and I went for a walk in Central Park afterwards. I felt as if I had wings, not fearing the dark places under the bridges in the Harlem district.

Anne became very talkative during our long walk. I asked her what happened the night at the jazz club, when she asked a stranger to dance. She said that she had invited him to her house and they had a shower together.

Exhausted from our walk, we had a horrendous dinner at a place called Polonia, and had coffee at Anne's apartment afterwards. I was curious to hear what had happened after the shower with the stranger. The story she told me about her love affair with a black woman called Ruth was far more interesting then her sexual encounter with that stranger.

Anne read some of Ruth's poems to me. One was about her cousin who had been poor as a child, had been a prostitute and died soon after she became a famous soprano.

Anne's voice became soft and tender as she read her own poems. They were about her passionate love for Ruth, their erotic life and intimate feelings, but Ruth left one day for a seductive Brazilian woman.

After Anne's love affair ended she became depressed and suicidal. She felt there was no hope until she went to that Harlem church.

We will go back to that church together next Sunday.

I had a dream last night. A small colored butterfly was flickering around me.

Suddenly the butterfly became sick, one of her little wings was broken.

I took her gently between my fingers, and she slowly, very slowly, stopped the flickering, and stopped moving.

She withered silently in my hand, like a dead flower.

The Barbizon — Wednesday

Crazy women in the corridors. Old glories of the past, left with no money, fearing to be sent to the streets.

Suicides were frequent. One had to watch out, when leaving the building: some woman might jump from a window, and land on your head. The elevator man, Jim, had always to be the witness.

He was tired and angry, when a woman had just thrown herself off the terrace. "They even come from Chicago to kill themselves in this building".

There was an elderly woman who always got my attention when she came for breakfast at the cafeteria. It was a funny picture seeing her. She dressed in rags, a sweater, skirt, stockings, and shoes full of holes held together with tape. She always dragged along two handbags and several bags, which were tied up with all sorts of cords and strings. She looked like an untidy parcel herself.

One day I asked Jim, the elevator man, about her. He became enraged, his eyes bulged out of their sockets. "That woman! Do you think that woman is poor? You would not believe it but she has a fortune. She walks around in rags only because she doesn't want anybody to know that she is rich. Do you know what I would do with that woman?" he continued shouting, as we ascended to my floor, "I would marry that old witch. I would take her to the beach one day, fill up a bag with sand and then hit her furiously on the head until she died." His eyes shined with satisfaction when he said this.

The peculiar elevator men at the Barbizon!

Only women were allowed on the floors. Once, there was a woman trying to get to the 5th floor. She was carrying a baby in her arms. "What is this?" the elevator man screamed, as he pointed to the child. "A boy or a girl?" The mother mumbled, "A boy, but he is only 8 months old." "No way ma'am, he cannot come into this hotel, only women allowed here."

Jim used to harass all the girls entering the elevator. We had to be very serious with him. He would make lecherous comments, bolstering himself as a macho man. It was very humiliating.

One day he looked very pale. He had a scared expression on his face. He approached me when I got into the elevator, and whispered in my ear: "Can you do me a favor. Please, can you ride up on the elevator with me to the upper floors, and then, I will drop you to your floor?" I was scared, but he looked terrified himself, for the first time. There were several women in the elevator, some old, some young and attractive. They left the elevator at different floors. We arrived at the 15th floor with only one other woman, when she left the elevator Jim made a great sigh. "Thank you, thank you very much," he said. "I asked you to accompany me because the last woman who got off is a nymphomaniac. She harasses me all the time whenever she is alone with me."

After that day, the elevator man never bothered us again.

Winter In Central Park — January

The first snow in New York. Here it is finally, the cold, freezing, slippery winter in New York. Boots and scarves, gloves and hats, umbrellas and warm, long, winter coats.

New York is suddenly clean. The white flakes cover the streets like a carpet. White, big white drops, pouring from the sky; the silence of the snow.

The squirrels are less shy in winter. They approach you and wait to be fed, sitting patiently on their big tails. They only run away when a dog approaches with bad intentions.

The children stare at The Delacorte Clock in the Zoo, which plays music every hour. They gaze at the bear, zebra and penguins dancing around the hours of time.

I remember a family of seals years ago. They were like a human family. The baby seal was very small then and wanted to get the attention of mommy and daddy who were leisurely resting on the rocks, their skin smooth and wet, absorbing the sun.

I didn't want to know what became of the seal's parents when I saw the lonely baby seal sliding through the waters like a snake.

I heard that someone had poisoned them. Some delinquent boys probably.

The dark part of the Central Park. The need to destroy, to kill.

I have seen teenagers in the park torturing animals. They were chasing the squirrels and trying to put them into sacks. Others threw stones at them. I noticed one squirrel watching me, he had one eye missing.

The beating of homosexuals in the night. They were attacked by youngsters with big sticks while they were cruising in the night. Some of them were beaten to death.

The cruelty of it all. The man and the beast. The beauty of nature, contrasting with the lower instincts of men turned loose.

LAST DAYS IN THE BARBIZON

New York — Monday

My memories. To dig into the past when the present is so painful to me. In my room at the Barbizon Hotel for Women, a small room which makes me feel claustrophobic. Longing for my space in Spain, my big rooms, hearing only the sound of singing birds. I can only hear the maddening sound of subway construction, the digging, my ears hurt me from the blast.

What keeps me from asking for another room? It will be worse. I know from experience another room will only be worse. It might have the heater just over my bed or pillow. There may be the shouting of some crazy woman in the corridor. There might be some smoky air, of a room drenched with tobacco, with sealed windows, keeping out the fresh air.

I was somehow able to write poetry in my room, despite being freezing cold. I recall a time when both windows became stuck open on one of the coldest days. I decided to be brave and ask the engineer to fix them. He fixed them so well that they became glued shut. The next day the temperature went up to 90 degrees and I thought I was in a sauna and was going to suffocate.

This year the old ladies have disappeared, dragging their poverty to a cheaper hotel where their complaints surely continue to be unheard. I somehow miss them. I felt ashamed of how I ignored them most of the time, wanting to concentrate on my writing. "Can I have a coffee with you?" they asked me frequently. Of course, I never refused.

They told me about how beautiful they used to be and about their success and glamour in their youth.

They were very nice to me and asked me about Spain, my photography show and my writing. But mostly they were dreamers. They mentioned their good connections and how they could introduce me to the curators of great galleries. I let them speak. I knew they were dreaming of their past, the old times, when success was around them, when they were praised for their youth, talent and money. The only contacts they had now were with the reception desk staff.

The unkindness of the receptionists at the Barbizon! When I talk to somebody at the reception desk, something freezes inside me, and I get the feeling of talking to unkind machines. I know they have a tough job and work many hours a day. They deal with as many complaints as there are rooms in this concentration camp for women. What they cannot be forgiven for is their unkindness to the old. They should pity the old, who are like defenseless children and need more human contact than bread to remain alive.

This jungle of human alienation that is New York City! To witness this, in the streets, in the busses and subways. The struggle for survival.

I saw a black man, a poor devil. Four policemen were not enough to restrain him. They crashed his head against the police car several times and twisted his feet. He was repeatedly brutalized, as if he were a wild beast. I couldn't help wondering what this man could have done to deserve such punishment. A hefty dose of tranquilizer would have been more effective than all the policemen's violence.

This fall the Barbizon has changed its face. It is painted bright colors. The curtains and bad covers have a new look, everything seems new and young.

Gone are the old ladies with their complaints and dreams of the past. Now there is youth. Young women sing in their rooms, some prepare their art exhibits, while others rehearse for a musical.

Since this youthful clientele is able to pay more, naturally the service at the reception desk has greatly improved. But the complaints are the same; they never end. One room is too warm, the other has no cold water running, and another still smells of the recent paint. This time it does not bother me that their complaints are unheard. The women are young and unlikely to get pneumonia when the wind blows in the half opened windows.

My fear of getting sick at the Barbizon has become an obsession. Not having insurance, I worry about the expenses of a doctor or clinic. I had about ten checkups in Spain before coming to New York. I haven't gotten sick this winter in New York. I have taken good care of myself and become my own doctor, nurse and therapist.

There is one thing, though, that I didn't foresee:
I fell in love in the spring.

NEW YORK —
THE EXCELL COFFEE SHOP

The Barbizon cafeteria is closed because of non-payment of rent. We all go to the Excell Coffee Shop, which is quite interesting too. The atmosphere is more human there. I am allowed to sit in a booth all by myself, at any time of day (not so at the Barbizon), and I write, think and observe the people coming in and out.

On the wall hang little plates that picture the Caryatids and the Parthenon. The owners and waiters are Greek. They all rush around now that the Barbizonian women have invaded the place.

When the waiters take the orders on the loud speaker, there accent is funny. "Sc-rrr-ambled eggs with ssaugsses," they scream. These young Greek men are converted into machines, twenty hands and arms carrying sandwiches and fried potatoes, rushing, rushing, sometimes sipping some cold coffee or soup on their way to the tables. These young men have left behind in Greece their families, their landscape and their skies, hoping to have a better living in America.

A crazy woman comes in from the cold. She is rocking all the time, like an autistic child, in a world of her own, far away from reality. I wanted to talk to her and sink deep into her mind and pull her out of her loneliness, I didn't move. I timidly observed her. Where does she live? Where is her family? I hear the waiter telling her, "Well, what can you do about it, you want food and you have no money. You cannot get food without money."

My mind wanders to the clean, cozy kitchens of the bistros in Greece, each member of the family preparing homemade dishes of moussaka, shish kabob, and tasty yogurts.

I remember the shoe polisher on the Greek island of Kos. While he was shining my friend's shoes, he talked about the war and how the Turks had tortured and raped Greek women. When he finished polishing the shoes, he invited us for a drink of Ouzo. This poor, old man inviting us! The give and take. We had given him the warmth of our attention, and he had given us the hospitality of old times. The drinks he offered us were more expensive then the cost of the shoe polish, but he would have been offended if we had not accepted. In Greece, one can never refuse an invitation for Ouzo, even if it is the middle of a sunny afternoon.

One day, walking in the streets of Samos, two wrinkled women, showing only some front teeth, came shouting at us in very loud voices. We could not understand what they were saying. Were they angry at us? Suddenly we realized they were offering us the tarts, precious gifts that they had been baking, since it was an important Greek holiday.

A rugged, unshaven young man enters the cafeteria. He can hardly make it to the counter. I am afraid of that strange looking beggar. His eyes look through you without seeing. The waiter was going to send him away, but the cashier stopped him and asked the man, "Do you have money?" The man nodded and was given some hot coffee and a danish to take out. His hands trembled when he paid the cashier. But he had money, the necessary money, to get through living that day.

Memories of Greece:

The small island of Kythira. We had arrived there by plane and a taxi driver showed us around the island. We asked him where we could have lunch. To our surprise, he invited us to his private home. We had the most exquisite meal on the patio of the house, under a huge fig tree. Black olives, tomatoes, bread and cheese, and homemade honey. The taxi driver's whole family joined us and we drank Retsina, and we laughed and sang with them.

The smiling faces in Greece! The fragrance of pine trees, the strong sun. The clear, refreshing waters of the sea. The warm weather, never a cloud in the sky. And olives and feta cheese and Greek salad in the shade of the fig tree. Feelings of being part of the earth, of the blues, of the sky.

From the window of the Greek cafeteria I watch the snow falling in big, heavy flakes...

I am still in New York, enjoying the magic of this city.

Very soon I will return to my Mediterranean country, to my family and friends. And swim in the blue seas of Barcelona and the Costa Brava.

But I will never forget the vitality of Manhattan, its skyscrapers in the misty gray, the small lights twinkling like tiny stars.

I feel happy in New York this winter night!

NEW YORK —
LAST DECADE OF THE EIGHTIES

New York — 31 December 1989

<u>Tomorrow 1990</u>.

A new start. Life renovates itself. Spring will soon come and an aroma of lilacs will invade the air.

And new dreams will appear, new hopes, new springs.

Sun, sun shining brightly; my gloomy mood has been fading away like a light smoke in the air.

I feel richer, I feel happy today, full of energy and hope.

To be alive! To immerse myself in the wonders of nature.

To be born again, fresh and new, my imagination loose, always asking why, always admiring the new.

A new decade is coming.

And we will discover more and more the mysteries of Nature.

We will worship it, like the ancient Indians.

We will worship the sun again, and the moon, and the changing seasons.

And admire every single bird that greets us in the morning.

We will join together with new hopes and prayers, and the color of the races will blend like different flags.

We will not kill anymore our brothers on earth, but will discover ways of alleviating human hunger and of being happier ourselves and then making others happier.

We will deepen our understanding of the human brain, since this is the most important gift that we receive from the time we are born.

We will learn how to transmit to others the energies of our being, and vitalize our surroundings with our thoughts and minds.

We will try to learn the best profession we can study: how to live life in its full.

These are the hopes for the decades to come!

The end of my diary
New York City, 31 December 1990

Josefina Fontanals Martí was born and brought up in Barcelona, where she studied languages and literature. However, because of a special interest in social psychiatry, in 1958 she decided to go to New York City, where she enrolled in Columbia University and received her degree in that field. She stayed in New York for seven years, doing social work in Spanish Harlem.

On returning to Barcelona, her life was to change when she visited an exhibition of Japanese photography. She became totally immersed in this art form and exhibited her work in various locations in Catalonia; New York City; and Oxford, England. Also, her interest in cinema led her to study script writing.

Once again she went to New York and enrolled in the liberal arts program at the New School for Social Research in 1980. After her graduation, she continued studying there and, in general, thrived on the accessible world of writers, psychiatrists and painters in the New York of the 80s. Since 1999 she has lived permanently in Barcelona, dedicating her time to the appreciation of art, literature, and nature. She has published two books in Spanish, *Diarios de una Adicta a Nueva York* and *Los Aparecidos*.